AVA'S BLESSING IN DISGUISE

A BLUSHING BRIDES SHORT STORY

LORANA HOOPES

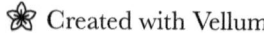

NOTE FROM THE AUTHOR

I have been so blessed to meet amazing authors in my journey, and I am excited to be joining with a few of them to bring you The Blushing Brides Christian Romance Series.

This book took on a life of its own when my readers told me they wanted a look at Justin and Ava in the future. I wondered what to write about, but after I suffered a medical scare, I figured my story would make a good story for Ava. If you would like to know more of my story, be sure to read the Author's Note at the end.

I hope you love this story of Justin and Ava. If you do, please leave a review at your retailer. It really does make a difference because it lets people make an informed decision about books.

The other books in the Blushing Bride series:
The Cowboy's Reality Bride

The Reality Bride's Baby

The Producer's Unlikely Bride

The Cop's Fiery Bride

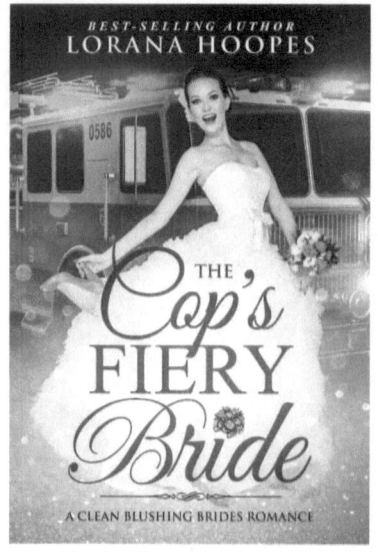

The Soldier's Stalwart Bride

BEST-SELLING AUTHOR
LORANA HOOPES

THE
Soldier's
STEADFAST
Bride

A BLUSHING BRIDES MARRIAGE
OF CONVENIENCE ROMANCE

*A*va rubbed the right side of her neck as she glanced over at her daughter spread eagle in the bed next to her. At four years of age, Kylie normally slept the entire night in her own bed, but for some reason, every night this week she had woken up screaming between three thirty and four thirty. Ava had dutifully walked down the hall and brought the girl back to her bed. Kylie wasn't the easiest person to sleep with as she tended to kick and punch, but Ava got more sleep that way than if she tried to stretch out in the recliner in Kylie's room.

"I sure wish I knew why she keeps waking up," Justin said rubbing his eyes. His voice was heavy with sleep. "I could use some decent sleep."

"Me too. I pray every night for her to sleep

through the night." Ava brushed blond curls from Kylie's forehead. "It must be a phase though."

As she rolled over, her hand stole back to her neck and rubbed the aching part again. She must have slept on it funny. Oh well, she'd call her massage therapist later. He was always telling her to come in more often anyway.

"Whoa, what happened to you?" Heidi, her friend and nanny, asked as Ava dropped Kylie off that morning. She'd met Heidi at the day care center she and Justin had chosen three years ago when Ava had decided to go back to writing full time. She loved spending time with Kylie at home, but she'd quickly realized she got no writing done when she had the baby all day, so they had agreed to put Kylie in a center for a few hours so Ava could get work done.

The center had been wonderful, but Heidi had been her favorite employee and when she decided to leave to start her own home center, Ava had willingly followed. Now, she was more like Kylie's aunt and a member of Ava's family than a nanny.

Ava's face scrunched in discomfort and her hand massaged her neck again. "I think I slept on it wrong.

When Kylie woke me up this morning – early again," she shot her daughter a pointed look, "I noticed it when I tried to go back to sleep."

Heidi nodded as she pulled a tray of blueberry muffins from the oven. "She took a long nap yesterday."

"Yeah, I don't know why she's been waking up in the middle of the night, but it's making for a long week." Ava yawned and covered her mouth.

"Well, I hope you get some work done today. Kylie give mommy a hug before she has to go."

"Bye Mommy," Kylie said as she wrapped her little arms around Ava's neck.

"Bye Baby. Be good for Heidi." Ava placed a kiss on her daughter's cheek before heading back to her car. As she climbed inside, a sharp pain shot down her neck. She punched in James's number and put the phone on speaker as she backed out of Heidi's driveway.

"Hey Ava, what can I do for you?" James had been her massage therapist for the last few years. Ava had never realized how much stress she carried in her shoulders until her pregnancy with Kylie. When she'd began suffering from headaches, her doctors had finally told her it was due to the stress in her shoulders. They had referred her to a massage therapist, and she had seen James once a month since then.

"James, I know it's a little early for my regular appointment, but I seemed to have tweaked my neck in my sleep. Is there any chance you have an opening today?"

"I don't think I have anything until after five, but let me check." Ava heard the clacking of computer keys before James came back on the line. "Sorry, Ava. Five pm is my first opening today."

"Okay thanks for checking." Five wouldn't work. Justin was filming today, so she'd have Kylie after three and Kylie would not sit through an hour-long massage. The girl was well-behaved but not that well-behaved. Surely, if she had Gen massage it a little bit, the pain would go away. She'd better stop and get Gen a coffee then. Butter her up a bit.

"To what do I owe this?" Gen asked as Ava placed the tall Caramel Macchiato on her desk.

Ava flashed her most charming, hopeful smile. "I was hoping you would massage my neck a little. I woke up with this slight stiffness and James can't get me in today."

Gen smiled and picked up the cup. "I would have done it for free, but thanks for the coffee." She took a sip before motioning Ava to sit at her desk. "What did you do?" she asked as her hands pressed on Ava's neck.

"I don't know. Slept on it wrong maybe. Kylie was up early again this morning and I noticed it when I tried to go back to sleep." Ava winced as Gen's fingers found the tender spot.

"You should go see Chris. I bet he could adjust you and get this taken care of." Chris was Gen's boyfriend who just happened to be a chiropractor.

"That's a good idea."

"Let me get you his number. I don't mind continuing to work on you, but I'd feel better if a professional looked at you." Gen grabbed a sticky note off Ava's deskpad and scribbled a number on it. "Call Chris."

"Okay, I will." Ava stuck the note on the side of her monitor. She didn't mind chiropractors – she'd been once or twice before – but she wasn't convinced that what they did helped. Maybe if she just tried writing, the pain would disappear and she could avoid going.

She pulled up her current work in progress and read over what she had typed the day before. It was so tempting to work at home, but she'd promised herself when Kylie came along that she would be present when she was home, so she kept her writing mainly for at the office and the occasional evening when she was awake after Kylie went to bed. That wasn't too many nights.

A rambunctious four-year-old not only kept Ava on her toes but wore her out, so that by the time Kylie was lying down, Ava was too exhausted to open her computer. The effect had been that her books took a little longer to release, but it had also forced her to plan them out better so that she didn't waste any writing time.

After she finished reading her words from yesterday, she glanced over her plot line. Ah, yes, that's where she was planning to go next. Her fingers stroked the keys and then the rhythmic tapping began. She grew so focused on the story that the pain in her neck lessened to a dull ache at least until she hit her first wall.

When she removed her fingers and leaned back, the pain reared its ugly head. It was worse than before, and now in addition to the pain, her neck felt stiff. Ava turned it to the right surprised to feel a sharp pain. She tried the left but got the same result. Okay, she might have to give Chris a call after all.

CHAPTER 2

*A*va pulled into the small parking lot of Chris's chiropractic office and parked the car. He had agreed to squeeze her in just before lunch, and she'd taken the appointment. A pain in the neck was one thing, but a stiff neck made her job so much harder.

"Welcome to Caring Chiropractic," the woman behind the desk said as Ava entered. "I'm Virginia."

"Ava Miller. I called ahead to see Chris er Dr. Gibson."

Virginia smiled. "Ah, yes. I have you on the books. Since it's your first time seeing us, I will need you to fill out some paperwork though."

"Of course." Ava had expected nothing less.

Everyone wanted forms filled out nowadays, but she supposed she couldn't blame them. With all the lawsuits in the world, it was especially important to have bases covered if you were in the medical profession.

She took the clipboard and the forms to one of the chairs in the small waiting room and began answering the questions. No, she wasn't injured on the job. At least she didn't think she had been. Yes, the pain was severe. No, it wasn't traveling down her arms or legs. Yes, it was hindering movement. No, she'd had no recent surgeries. In fact, the last time she had been in the hospital was Kylie's birth. No, she had not been in an accident. She circled the area on the diagram that corresponded with her pain and flipped the form over. After reading the legalese, she signed her name consenting to treatment and then returned the clipboard to the desk.

"Ava, if you want to follow me, I'll do a quick consultation before Dr. Gibson sees you."

Ava followed the petite blond woman down the hall to a small room. It held only the adjusting table, a stool, and one chair. Virginia sat down in the stool and motioned for Ava to take the chair. "You drove yourself, right?"

"Yes, though I'm not sure I should have. I had

motion this morning, but now my neck is so stiff I can barely turn it." Ava attempted to demonstrate but the pain kept her from turning very much.

"That's fine. I just see that your insurance company requires in house x-rays and Dr. Gibson will want some before he treats you. Do you think you could drive to their clinic and then back here?"

The thought sounded as appealing as getting a root canal, but if it would stop the pain, Ava would do it. "I don't think it's very safe for me to be driving far, but as it's right down the road, I could probably do it."

"Is there someone who could drive you?"

"Yeah, maybe Genevieve. I'll call her and see if she can meet me here."

"Great. I'll put in the order and we'll get you taken care of."

Ava followed Virginia back to the front and while she placed the order, Ava shot off a text to Gen. A few minutes later, Gen entered the office, a harried frown on her face.

"Why didn't you tell me it had gotten worse?" Gen asked as she helped Ava into her Range Rover.

"It came on kinda suddenly. I was working on the book and when I stopped typing, I realized my neck had stiffened." Ava let out a groan as Gen hit a bump in the road.

"Sorry, I'll slow it down and watch for bumps."

Ava closed her eyes and sent a prayer up as Gen continued to drive. 'Lord, please take this pain away. Let it be nothing major and give the doctors the wisdom to fix it.'

"We're here," Gen said a moment later and Ava eased herself out of the car.

Radiology was on the first floor of the clinic and it took only a few minutes to get checked in, but by the time they sat down, Ava's head felt as if it weighed an extra fifty pounds. She leaned over, letting it rest lightly on her hands. It wasn't extremely comfortable, but it eased a little of the burden from her neck.

"Ava Miller?"

"Here." Ava said the word without looking up. That would follow but slowly. "Guess I'll be right back," she said to Gen before following the woman into the bowels of radiology.

"Okay, it looks like we're taking three cervical x-rays today, so I need you to remove your shirt, bra, and any jewelry on your neck or ears." The woman pointed to a folded piece of fabric on a stool.

"There's a gown here. Go ahead and put it on but don't worry about tying it. I'll help you with that."

Ava chuckled. She couldn't have tied anything behind her back at the moment if she tried. In fact, she wasn't entirely sure she'd be able to get her shirt and necklace off, but she'd deal with that if it happened.

The woman pulled the curtain closed behind her and Ava took a deep breath before peeling her shirt off. The necklace was a little easier as she was able to turn the clasp to the front of her neck and not have to reach so far, but she wasn't sure she would bother putting it back on. However, she held the golden cross for a moment and whispered another prayer for healing and knowledge before laying it on her shirt. Then she slid her bra off, added it to the pile, and put on the gown.

"Ready?" the technician asked as Ava pulled open the curtain.

"I think so." Ava turned so the woman could tie the back and then she followed the woman into the darkened room just ahead.

"Okay, can you put your left shoulder against this and then hold still?"

"That shouldn't be a problem since I can barely move," Ava said with a small smile.

"I'm so sorry. Hopefully we can figure out what's going on and get you fixed up." The woman moved another piece of the x-ray machine closer to Ava's right side and then disappeared into a small room. Ava heard a hum followed by a beep and then the woman reappeared. "Okay, now if you can put your back against this."

Ava did as she was told but she couldn't get the back of her head completely against the piece the technician pointed to. "Here let me help." The woman pushed gently on Ava's forehead until it rested against the back part. Ava grimaced only slightly and tried not to let the fear overtake her. What was wrong with her?

"Hold there." The woman disappeared again. Another hum, beep, and the woman appeared again. "Okay, last one. It's going to sound weird, but I need you to open your mouth."

Ava had no idea what that position helped them see, but she complied and then the experience was over.

"You need to take these back, correct?"

"Yes ma'am."

"Great. Go ahead and get dressed and head back to the lobby. I'll get them copied to a disk and should have it ready in about five minutes."

"Thank you." Ava stepped back into the small room that held her clothing and redressed placing her necklace in her pocket. Then she headed back to the lobby. As soon as she reached the chair next to Gen, she once again let her head rest on her hands. It felt so heavy and stiff.

Gen placed a hand on her shoulder but said nothing. Ava didn't mind. The gesture alone brought a comfort that words couldn't have anyway.

"Here you are," the technician said a few minutes later and handed Ava an envelope.

Ava tucked it in her purse and thanked the technician before following Gen back to her car.

"Will you be okay if I drop you off?" Gen asked as she fastened her seatbelt. "I need to run some errands."

"Yeah, I'll be fine. I'll probably go home after this and it isn't far." Ava had no idea how the adjustment would go, but it had to be better than what she was feeling now. She rested her head against the headrest in the car and prayed they wouldn't hit any bumps.

When they arrived back at the chiropractor's, Gen helped Ava out of the car. "Be sure to let me know how it goes," she said as she opened the front door for Ava.

"I will, thank you." Ava waved to her friend and

then stepped up to the front desk. She handed the envelope to Virginia and then took a seat again.

"Let me just get these loaded up, Ava, and I'll be right back."

"I'll be here," Ava said but she didn't lift her head. It felt better if she could just let her hands hold the weight up.

Virginia disappeared down the hallway, but a moment later she was back again muttering under her breath. "I can't believe they did that. Angela, can you get Radiology on the line for me?"

Uh oh, this didn't sound good. Ava hoped they didn't want her to drive back because she didn't think she would be able to.

"Hi, this is Virginia over at Caring Chiropractic. I just sent a patient over for x-rays. She brought back the film but it's encrypted. I tried her date of birth but that isn't opening it... No, I can't open any part of it... I don't know what to tell you, it says it's encrypted... Okay, well, thank you."

"What's the problem?" Chris's voice joined the conversation.

"They sent the films but they're encrypted. The guy at Ava's clinic just told me that they don't do that. He refused to help me."

"Let's just do the x-rays in house free of charge.

If we don't charge for them, we aren't breaking the insurance company's rules."

Ava wanted to thank him. There was no way she could have driven back to the clinic.

"Ava? Come with me?" Ava stood and followed Virginia down the hallway once again. "I'm so sorry about this."

"I'm just glad you have the option to do them in house. I don't think I could have driven back."

Virginia rolled her eyes. "No, and it's ridiculous that that's what they wanted you to do. We'll just get these taken quickly and get you some relief."

"Thank you." Ava followed Virginia's directions and stood still while the x-rays were taken again.

"All right, Ava, all done. Dr. Gibson should be in soon."

Ava sank down in the chair and rested her head once again. She hoped Chris would be able to provide her relief. The pain was getting more intense.

The door opened and Chris entered. "Hey Ava. I'm sorry to see you're in so much pain. You have no idea what you did, huh?"

"No, I just woke up with a slight pain in my neck, but now I can't move it."

"It's probably a pinched nerve, but let me take a look at your x-rays."

Ava used her fingers to tilt her head up slightly so she could see the screen. She had no idea how to read the pictures, but even she could tell that the top vertebrate in her neck didn't look right.

"Yep, right there." Chris pointed at the twisted vertebrate. "Your C1-C4 are very clearly out of alignment. The good news is we can treat you and get you some relief. The bad news is that it's going to take a few days."

The weight that sat on Ava's shoulders grew heavier. "Days?"

"Yeah, I mean I would bet that you'll be about ten percent better tomorrow and another twenty percent the day after. Then when we have you moving again, we can look at why this happened. Okay?"

"Okay." Ten percent wasn't much, but Ava's pain was so bad now that she would take whatever relief he could give. Even if it was only ten percent.

"Now this is going to hurt today, but it should feel a little better after this adjustment." He held out a hand to help her stand and led her over to the adjustment table. "Let's have you lie down on your back."

"I'm not sure I can," Ava said in a small voice.

"I'll help. Just wrap your arms around my neck."

Ava did as Chris instructed, and he placed a hand behind her neck. The pain hit when she was still a foot from the table and by the time he got her prone, tears filled her eyes.

"I know this hurts and what I'm about to do will hurt even more, but then you should feel better." His hands twisted and pulled at her neck and Ava bit back the scream that wanted to emerge. "Wiggle your left foot," he said and then yanked on her neck.

Pain like she had never felt before flooded her body, and Ava couldn't stop the whimper that escaped her lips. Nor could she stop the tear that trickled out of the corner of her eye.

"I know. One more."

Ava wasn't sure she could take one more, but before she had time to think about it, he had probed and yanked the right side of her neck. The pain burned through her body blacking out her vision for a moment. More tears joined the first cascading down her cheeks.

"I know it hurts, and it's okay to cry. I'll be right back with an ice pack, and I just want you to lay here for twenty minutes or so."

Ava wasn't sure she could stay in this position another five minutes much less twenty, but she would try. As Chris left the room to get the ice pack, Ava let the tears stream down her face. "Please, Lord, take the pain away."

Chris returned a moment later with the ice pack and slid it under her neck before exiting again, but the pain didn't lessen. Ava felt trapped. She couldn't sit up due to the pain, but she couldn't lay here much longer. Should she scream out? Could they hear her crying? Surely, he would come back in a few minutes. She could last another few minutes.

"How are you doing?" Chris asked a few minutes later as he entered the room again.

"Can I sit up and put the ice on my neck that way?" Ava managed through her tears.

"It's not quite as effective. Is this position bothering you?"

"It hurts so much."

"Okay, let's get you up then."

Ava had no strength to even help push; she was completely reliant on Chris as he put an arm around her and pulled her up. Again, the pain blacked out her vision for a moment.

"There you go. Think you're okay to drive home?"

"Maybe in a minute. The room is still spinning."

"Of course. When you get home, I want you to sit

with this ice pack on. Twenty minutes on and then chill it for forty. Then ice again. Okay?"

Ava agreed but she was beginning to wonder if she would make it home. And if she did, how she would venture out again to get Kylie. She was going to have to call in more favors.

CHAPTER 3

*J*ustin's face was etched with concern when he entered the house that night. "Ava? What's going on?"

She put her fingers to her lips and pointed to Kylie who was curled up on the couch. With a much softer voice she answered his question. "I'm not sure. I woke up a little stiff today and now I can't move my neck."

"Have you been to the doctor?"

"I went and saw Chris. He thinks it's just a pinched nerve."

Justin folded his arms across his chest and raised an eyebrow. "No offense to Chris, but I think you need to see a doctor. What if it's something more serious?"

"I have another adjustment with him tomorrow, but if it's not better, I promise I'll go to the doctor. Now, do you think you can take this little one upstairs to her bed? I'm probably going to sleep here tonight." The painful memory of trying to lay flat at the chiropractor's was still fresh in her mind and Ava had no desire to repeat that. Plus, Justin left earlier in the morning than she did. What if she could lay down but then couldn't get up the next morning? No, it was better to sleep in the recliner and not bother Justin. Besides, the pain was manageable as long as she sat just perfectly in the recliner.

"Yes, I'll get Kylie, and then I'm coming back to check on you."

Ava appreciated his concern, but there was nothing he could do for her. She'd spent the last several hours icing her neck, then sleeping while it chilled again, then icing it again. Afraid to drive more than she had to, she'd asked Gen to pick up Kylie and grab her some food on the way home. Thankfully, Kylie had been willing to spend the evening watching TV on the couch – something Ava rarely let her do most days.

True to his word, Justin returned after scooping Kylie up and dropping her off upstairs. "Is there anything I can do for you?" His eyes roamed over Ava as if unsure where or how to help.

"Can you put this back in the freezer for me?" She handed him the ice pack and grimaced only slightly as her neck readjusted to the slight difference in space with the pack gone.

He took it from her and walked to the kitchen. She heard the freezer door open and close, and then he was in front of her again. "Anything else?"

"Pray with me?" Though Ava had been praying throughout the day herself, hearing her husband pray over her sounded like exactly the healing she needed.

With a smile, Justin placed his hand on her head. "Lord, we thank you for this day. We thank you for the many blessings you have given us, but tonight we come to you with a request. Please heal Ava's neck – whatever is going on – and give her rest. We know that you are the divine healer and we ask that you would place that healing hand on her. Give her comfort and healing so that she can return to her normal life. In your name we pray, Amen."

"Amen," Ava echoed and she squeezed his hand. "Thank you. I'm sorry I won't be in bed tonight."

Justin leaned down and placed a kiss on her forehead. "You just worry about you and getting the rest you need. Besides if I get too lonely, there's a couch right there I can come claim."

"I love you, Justin Miller."

"And I love you, Ava." He placed another kiss on her cheek and then headed upstairs.

Ava was left in the dark empty living room. Justin often fell asleep down here when he got off work late, but Ava never did, and the eerie quiet pressed in on her. She flicked on the TV and surfed through the channels until she found something she wouldn't mind watching.

At some point her eyes closed, and when she opened them again, the show was over. The clock showed an hour had passed and as Ava's neck was throbbing again, she decided to get the ice pack once more. And maybe some Tylenol. Chris had suggested she go light on the pain killers so that she didn't assume she was better and tweak her neck even more, but at this point Ava doubted two Tylenol would do that for her. She wasn't even sure how much it would dull the pain, but she needed something.

She shuffled into the kitchen and retrieved the ice pack wrapping it in a paper towel to keep it from burning her neck. Then she grabbed the Tylenol from the upper cabinet. Kylie wasn't the type of kid to get into cabinets, but Ava still liked keeping the medicine out of her reach.

Ava flicked the lid off easily but as she stared down at the two white pills in her palm, she wondered how she was going to swallow them. Taking pills was not her specialty and the only way she could generally do it was to fill her mouth with water, tilt her head back, and drop the pills in. But there was no way she could do that in her current condition. She'd have to try something different.

Ava filled her mouth with water and then as carefully as possible, she slid the pills into her mouth. When they were both in, she swallowed, hoping the water would wash them down her throat. She hated the bitter taste of pills in her mouth if they didn't make it down the first time. Thankfully, luck was with her and she felt both pills make it down her throat. After replacing the pill bottle, she grabbed the ice pack and headed back to the recliner.

It took her another few minutes, but finally she was situated just right so that the pain was manageable and she was as comfortable as possible.

"MOMMY, CAN I HAVE CEREAL?"

Ava opened her eyes and turned as much as she could to see her daughter standing next to the recliner. "Yeah Baby. Just give Mommy a second to wake up." A second wouldn't really cut it. Nor would a pot of black coffee. Ava had tossed and turned most of the night either waking up due to the pain or some unknown creak and groan of the house. She would definitely be napping today after getting Kylie dropped off.

Her neck screamed in agony as she righted the recliner and stood. Ava had thought that maybe it was getting a little better yesterday with all the icing, but this morning it seemed even stiffer if that was possible, and a funny pressure in her ears along with a fire when she swallowed had joined the pain in her neck. But she put on a brave face for her daughter.

"Did you sleep good Pumpkin?" She ruffled her daughter's blond curls as she crossed to the kitchen.

"Yeah, I didn't dream though."

"Well, we don't always dream, so that's not always a bad thing. Did you want cereal this morning?"

"Uh huh, the cinnamon kind."

Ava retrieved a bowl and then grabbed the cereal from the pantry. With her daughter taken care of, she turned her attention to the coffee pot. She had never drunk coffee until she met Justin, but his pot a day habit had started to slowly rub off on her, and now she found she craved a cup or two in the morning. Thankfully, her stomach seemed to hit its coffee limit at two cups which was usually fine with Ava. Today though she wished it would tolerate more because she wasn't sure how she would function on just two cups.

"Are you going to take a shower today, Mommy?" Kylie asked before shoveling in a large spoonful of cereal.

Ava grimaced at the thought. It had been hard enough washing her hair yesterday morning and she'd had limited movement then. She had none today and couldn't imagine how challenging it would prove this morning. "I think I'll skip it today. Mommy has to take off work today and rest anyway."

Kylie's face lit up. "Can I stay home with you Mommy?"

"Oh, baby, I'd love that, but Mommy has to go see the doctor again to see if he can fix my neck. Then I'll probably sleep most of the day. I wouldn't be much fun today."

Kylie's lips pushed out in a pout. "Okay, Mommy, but we'll have a playday soon, right?"

"Of course we will." Ava hoped she wasn't lying to her daughter. The thought of anything more than sitting in her chair all day sent her stomach curling in on itself, but surely another adjustment today would have her neck feeling better.

After a quick breakfast for herself and a change of clothes for both of them, Ava herded Kylie out to the car. "Can you climb up today, baby? Because Mommy cannot lift you."

"Sure I can, Mommy. I'm four now, remember?" Said in her matter of fact voice, Ava couldn't help but smile as she watched her daughter climb into the car. When had she gotten so big?

Ava eased herself into her own seat trying not to move her neck any more than she had to. The ride to Heidi's was slow and painful, but Ava once again thanked God when she arrived safely. Driving with limited movement was scary, but having her daughter in the car upped her anxiety. She would never forgive herself if she got in an accident with Kylie in the car.

"Whoa, you don't look much better," Heidi said as Ava signed Kylie in.

"No, I'm afraid it isn't much better. I couldn't even lay down last night – had to sleep in the recliner, but I have another adjustment today, so I'm hoping that helps."

"I'll be praying for you." Those five simple words were one of the main reasons Ava and Justin had followed Heidi when she started her in home center.

At the other daycare, most of the workers had been believers but because it was a business, they could rarely express their faith, but Heidi worked for herself now and that meant she could be open and vocal about her beliefs. Ava was comforted by the knowledge that Heidi would not only talk to Kylie about God but taught her prayers as well.

"Thank you." Ava glanced down at Kylie wrapped tightly around her leg. "Kylie, honey, it's time to stay with Heidi. She'll take good care of you until Mommy comes back."

"No, I don't want you to leave," Kylie said shaking her head back and forth.

"Kylie, you have to. Mommy has to get her neck fixed again, but I promise I'll be back to get you this afternoon."

"You promise?" Her daughter's wide blue eyes tugged on Ava's heart. She'd thought she was doing a good job hiding her pain, but clearly Kylie could sense something was off. Ava would have to up her game and work on her poker face to assure her daughter.

"I promise baby."

CHAPTER 4

*D*read filled Ava as she pulled into the parking lot of Caring Chiropractic. It wasn't that she disliked seeing Chris or even his employees, but the thought of the adjustment and the pain it would bring again was almost unbearable. She took a deep breath and prayed for courage as she opened the front door of the office.

"Ava, you look better today," Chris said.

"Really? I don't feel any better. I still can't move my neck and I had to sleep in a chair last night."

He nodded as if he'd expected that answer. "Not surprising, but after today's adjustment, you should feel thirty percent better."

Ava scribbled her name on the sign in log. "Is it going to hurt as much as it did yesterday?"

"Probably, but then it will get better. Come on, I'll take you back before you have too long to think about it." He motioned for her to follow him down the hallway.

"Do we have to do it lying down again?" The fear in Ava's voice surprised her. She didn't normally consider herself a fearful person, but that pain yesterday had been... she didn't even have words for what it had been.

"We can try sitting if you'd like." Chris pulled the chair into the center of the room and patted the back. "Just make sure you put your back all the way against the back of the chair here."

Ava complied and tried to relax as his hands felt around her neck again, but it was impossible. Even with his help in moving her neck, the pain started before he yanked and then skyrocketed off the charts with the swift movement. Not quite as bad as yesterday but close. Oh, so close. The second yank sent tears to her eyes but they didn't fall today.

"Okay, more ice today and take it easy." Chris patted her shoulder and then helped her stand.

"I will." Ava had no plans to do anything other than sit in her recliner, sleep, and maybe write a little if she was lucky.

❦

WHEN SHE WOKE THAT AFTERNOON, the first thing she did was pop more Tylenol. She didn't like feeling like she needed it to get through the day, but that's exactly where she was.

The Tylenol dulled the ache enough that she decided to try writing. She settled into the chair and opened her laptop, but before she dove into her story, she decided to check her mail. Normally an everyday activity, she hadn't done it at all yesterday.

Ava sighed as she read the first email. She was supposed to lead worship practice tonight. Having always loved singing, she had joined the worship team shortly after she and Justin married. And she loved it, but the thought of singing on stage this week with such pain in her neck filled her with fear. She should cancel, say she couldn't make it, but the normal worship leader and the pianist were both out of town. The responsibility for making sure the team practiced and sounded good lay firmly on her shoulders.

She'd have Justin drive her tonight. He'd said he'd be home earlier today. Dropping Kylie off was scary enough but Heidi's home was close so she didn't have to drive far. The church was across town and would require getting on the interstate – not something Ava felt comfortable doing with no movement in her neck. And surely by Sunday the pain would be gone or at least diminished enough that she could function.

With her game plan figured out, Ava finished checking the mail and then loaded her work in progress. The words came easily enough but fatigue hit with them, and by early afternoon, she was fairly certain she had slept more than she had written.

"HEY BABY, let's get you in the car. You get to come to worship practice with Mommy tonight." Ava forced a cheeriness in her voice that she didn't feel but hoped would relieve any fears that Kylie might be feeling.

Kylie's eyes lit up and she clapped her hands together. "Can we watch you sing?"

"Sure, baby, if it's okay with Daddy." Ava glanced Justin's direction and he nodded.

"Might as well since we are your ride."

"Thank you for this," Ava said lowering her voice so Kylie wouldn't overhear. "I just didn't want to chance anything having to drive so much farther."

"It's my pleasure. I don't need anything happening to you." He planted a quick kiss on her cheek before ushering them out the door.

Ava tried not to grimace during the ride to the church. On one hand, she was glad Justin was driving so she didn't have to move her neck, but he was a much more aggressive driver than she was and he didn't avoid the bumps or slow down on the turns which also aggravated her pain. Relief flooded her when the car stopped and the engine turned off.

"Mommy, come get me," Kylie hollered from behind Justin's seat.

"Baby, I wish I could, but Daddy is going to have to get you today." This was what Ava hated the most - not being able to function normally, not being able to pick up her daughter. "But I'll hold your hand once he gets you down."

"Okay." Resignation filled Kylie's voice, but she didn't fight them.

Justin and Kylie sat dutifully in the front row of the church while Ava led worship. The pain never left, but an odd tingling sensation trickled across her head as she sang the words to God. Perhaps just lifting her praises to God in this way would bring the healing she sought.

CHAPTER 5

*A*va woke even stiffer Friday morning. How was that possible? Shouldn't two adjustments have helped if it was a pinched nerve? Did that mean it was something more serious? Something she should worry about?

Amazed she had been able to sleep in the bed instead of the recliner, Ava braced for the pain as she pushed herself upright. Sure enough, it washed over her, a tidal wave of tightness, stiffness, and the feeling of a knife jabbing into the right side of her neck. It took a moment for the blackness to fade and the room to stay still enough that she could stand.

A shower sounded like the most painful thing on Earth at the moment, but she hadn't taken one yesterday. Two days was her limit. Even after Kylie had been born, she'd snuck into the bathroom and given herself as much of a shower as she could the second day much to the chagrin of the nurse who found her there. She'd taken a tongue lashing and been forced to promise she would call for help next time before she attempted a shower, but at least she had gotten clean. The gritty, slimy feeling had left her hair and taken the constant itch with it. And that was all Ava was hoping for today. Just enough clean to not feel gross.

She peeled off her clothes and stepped into the warm shower. The water pelted her neck but not in a painful way. Washing her hair, on the other hand, nearly brought her to tears. Unable to lean her head back, she backed closer to the shower head and let the water pour down her face. She scrubbed the soap out while trying to stay as still as possible and breathed a sigh of relief when the cleansing process was finished. But drying off was no less painful. Trying to dry her hair without moving her neck proved impossible and she stopped when the pain became unbearable. Her hair wasn't dry – far from it – but it could air dry the rest of the way.

"Mommy!" Kylie's yell came from down the hall. They had taken the railing off her bed a year ago, but she still refused to get up herself.

"Coming," Ava hollered back. Nothing like rushing to get dressed when you could barely move. She pulled on a pair of sweatpants and a loose-fitting shirt before heading down the hallway to Kylie's room. "Morning bug. You ready to get up?"

"Can I stay home with you today, Mommy?" Kylie asked as she sat up and rubbed her eyes. Her little stuffed lamb, once a pure white color but now loved to a dirty beige, was clasped tightly against her chest.

"Not today, baby, but it's Friday, which means tomorrow is Saturday and that's a stay home all day with Mommy day." Ava opened Kylie's drawers and pulled out her clothes for the day.

"Okay, Mommy."

Ava smiled as Kylie followed her downstairs. If only everyone was as accommodating and easy to please as her four-year old.

AVA DROPPED her keys on the table and sank into the recliner again. The third adjustment had been less painful, but Chris had promised she would have more movement and she still didn't. It still hurt to move her neck and swallow. Something else had to be going on.

As she pulled up her email, a message icon popped across her screen. Results from her x-rays had posted to her health account. Unsure she would understand the medical jargon but curious as to what it might say, she logged in and clicked on the medical record. The report wasn't long, but the words sent a spear of fear into her heart:

Impression: Unremarkable bony structures of the cervical spine. Nonspecific prevertebral soft tissue swelling from the C1 level to the C4 level. Clinical correlation for possible prevertebral infection is recommended. Consider CT neck with contrast to further evaluate. POSITIVE ALERT The results of this study have been annotated as abnormal in the patient's electronic medical record.

Prevertebral tissue swelling? What did that mean? Possible infection? CT scan? Abnormal? Suddenly, Ava was convinced this was not just a pinched nerve. She grabbed her cell phone and dialed the number to the clinic. Hopefully she hadn't made things worse by waiting so long to be seen. It was only two days. Surely two days wouldn't matter.

"Family health center, how may I direct your call?"

"I need to set an appointment to be seen," Ava said.

The woman transferred her to the right department and Ava rattled off the details of the x-ray report.

"I can get you in Monday morning with Dr. Stedman but that's the earliest appointment I have," the woman on the other end said apologetically.

"That's okay. I'll take it." But Ava wasn't going to wait another two days to be seen. Not with the words abnormal hanging over her head. She might have to sit there for hours, but her clinic had an Urgent Care department. At least she would get seen today. She tucked her laptop into her bag, grabbed her keys, and headed out for the second time.

The Urgent Care department was surprisingly slow when Ava arrived, and after being checked in, she was whisked quickly back into the triage room and then down the hall to a more permanent room. A nurse peppered her with questions before promising to return shortly with the doctor.

Ava sat in the chair and tried not to let fear overtake her. A few minutes later, a large, friendly black woman entered.

"Ava, I'm Dr. Jensen. I've looked over your results and I'm lining up a CT scan immediately. It may be nothing but infections in the neck are never something to mess with. Okay?"

"Whatever you suggest. I just want the pain to go away."

"We do need you to get on the bed. Erica needs to put an IV in because this CT will use an iodine contrast. Can you lie down?"

Ava sat on the edge of the bed. "Lying down is a little tough, but I'll try."

The doctor pushed a button to bring the head of the bed up so that it wasn't as much of an incline and Ava gratefully leaned back. The position still wasn't completely comfortable but it was much better than laying flat.

"All right, Erica will get you set up and then someone from the CT unit will be in to get you. I'll be back once I have results."

"Thank you."

Ava watched as the nurse inserted a needle into her veins and began to draw blood out. Normally, she hated having blood drawn but the pain was so minor compared to the aching in her neck that she didn't even care. After filling four vials, the nurse plugged in the piece that would attach to the IV and left the room.

Ava pulled out her cell phone and opened her book app. She couldn't write, but maybe she could pass the time reading. She rarely got to anymore since most of her free time was spent writing.

"Ava Miller?"

Ava glanced over at the door where a young woman stood with a wheelchair. "That's me." The woman helped get her situated in the wheelchair and then pushed her out the back doors of the clinic.

"I know it seems odd, but the CT scanners are housed in these mobile units. Don't worry though, they work just the same."

Ava would have nodded if she were able but as the statement didn't appear to require an answer, she didn't give one.

The woman maneuvered the wheelchair onto a ramp and then pressed a button to raise the ramp. When it stopped, she manually lifted the metallic closure and the interior of the trailer was exposed. It looked like a miniature lab with another technician manning a computer just outside of the white CT machine.

"Have you ever had a CT scan with contrast?" the technician asked her.

"I don't think so." Ava wasn't even sure she'd ever had a CT before much less with contrast.

"Are you allergic to iodine?"

"Not that I know of." What happened if she was?

Visions of her coding or going into some short of shock filled her mind and she closed her eyes to force them away. Sometimes having the imagination of a writer was a curse as much as a blessing.

"Can you lie back?" the woman asked.

"Not without help," Ava replied and the two flanked her and helped her lie back.

"Okay, now when the iodine hits, you're going to feel a warm sensation. It might even feel like you've wet yourself, but don't worry that's normal."

Ava wasn't sure how that could be normal but she said nothing.

"Be sure to keep your eyes closed throughout the procedure and there's a few times I'm going to ask you not to swallow."

No worries there. Swallowing was extremely painful and she avoided it at all costs. The bed she was on moved and Ava shut her eyes. A few minutes later, the CT scan was done. The technicians helped her back up and the woman who wheeled her out wheeled her back to her room.

Before climbing back in the bed, Ava grabbed her computer and placed it beside her along with her phone. She should have brought her charger in, but she couldn't imagine she would be here much longer.

She was wrong. It was an hour later when the

nurse finally returned. "Looks like I need a little more blood and then you need to get this antibiotic which takes about half an hour to administer."

"Antibiotic? So, it is an infection then?"

The nurse appeared thrown by the question. "Dr. Jensen hasn't been back in yet?"

"No one's been in for over an hour. I was beginning to think you'd forgotten about me."

"No, we haven't. I'll get you started and then check in with Dr. Jensen." The nurse filled a few more vials with blood and then fiddled with the IV plug for a minute until she appeared satisfied the IV was hooked up correctly. "Back in a bit," she said as she exited the room.

Ava sighed. An infection wasn't great news, but antibiotics generally cured them and at least it might mean faster relief for her neck.

"Oh good, Erica got you set up," Dr. Jensen said as she re-entered the room. "So, it does look like you have an infection in your neck. I'm glad you came in when you did. We don't want an infection like this getting into your bloodstream."

"How would I know if it got into my bloodstream?"

"You would probably have severe chills or fever. If

you have any of those signs, you need to go straight to the ER, not here, do you understand?"

"Yes ma'am."

"I'm prescribing you a strong antibiotic that you need to take for ten days along with a muscle relaxer and some pain medicine that you can take as needed. I want you to set a follow-up appointment for a week from now to make sure everything is improving."

"I can do that." Ava would do just about anything if it would lessen the pain she was feeling.

"Good. Erica will be back shortly with your discharge paperwork and your pharmacy papers. I hope you feel better soon."

So did Ava.

CHAPTER 6

*A*va woke with a start to the sun coming in her window. Ten am? How had she slept so long? Even though Saturday was a sleep in day, Kylie never let her sleep past eight. Justin must have gotten her before she could wake Ava up.

Ava tested her neck. It was definitely still stiff, but the throbbing seemed a little less today. Or was that just wishful thinking? Maybe, but it also hurt less to swallow and that she was not making up. It was the first time in days that swallowing didn't feel like someone squeezing her throat. Perhaps the medicine was working.

As she went to sit up though, the pain struck anew. Not as bad as yesterday but definitely not healed. Baby steps. She would need to do baby steps.

Ava rolled to her left side and then pushed herself up that way. Less pain, but the world still tilted for a minute. When it stopped, she continued into the bathroom and dressed for the day.

"How you feeling today, honey?" Justin asked as she stepped into the kitchen.

"Better. Not great yet, but better." She tilted her head but there was still little movement.

"Mommy, Daddy and I let you sleep in. Weren't we good?" Kylie asked appearing over the back of the couch.

"You were very good, baby. Mommy thanks you. Sleep is important for Mommy to heal. And so is breakfast." Ava poured herself a bowl of cereal and then a cup of coffee.

"We can just stay home today, right Mommy?"

"We can, but maybe you can let Mommy get a little writing done? I've been so tired that I haven't written much at all this week."

"Sure, I can do that."

Ava smiled at her daughter. Even when her life was turned upside down, she managed to keep a smile on her face and find the joy in the small things in life. If only adults could live life more like children.

In her pocket, her cell phone buzzed and Ava pulled it out curious as to who would be calling.

"Joyce? What can I do for you?" Joyce was the pianist and the boss of the worship team as far as Ava was concerned.

"I heard about your neck. If you need to take tomorrow to sleep, John can lead for you."

"Thank you. I started medication last night so I'm hopeful it will feel better, but if it's not better tonight, I promise I'll call you and John." Ava knew she probably should stay home, but she felt closest to God when she was on stage singing, and she hated giving that up. Unless her neck worsened today, she was sure she could make it through the three hours of church anyway.

"You don't think staying home would be a good idea?" Justin asked her after she ended the call.

"It might, but I feel like God asked me to lead for the same reason He asked me to write. I always feel like there's something He wants me to say. If I get nothing by tonight and the pain is any worse, I'll surrender."

Justin shot her a look full of disbelief, but he didn't argue. After five years of marriage, he knew when to push and when to step back, and Ava loved him even more for that. She planted a kiss on his cheek on her way to the sink where she deposited her dishes. Hopefully she would feel up to washing them later.

"Hey sleepyhead, you do any work anymore?"

Ava opened her eyes to see Gen standing over her. What time was it? Her neck felt stiff, but maybe that was just from the uncomfortable position of the recliner. "Sorry, Gen, I was working, but I guess I dozed off." She turned her wrist to see her watch and her eyes widened. It was nearly six? She'd slept through lunch and almost through dinner?

"I can see that. I brought some Chinese if you feel up to it."

"Mongolian Beef?" Ava asked hopefully. It was her favorite and Gen knew it.

"Of course. I would never show up without your favorite. I also have some Orange Chicken for Justin and some Sweet and Sour Chicken for little miss Kylie." She flashed a smile at Kylie who sat on the couch watching something on YouTube.

"You didn't let her watch TV all afternoon, did you?" Ava asked Justin as she righted the recliner and pushed herself up. She really needed her neck to heal so she could back to her routine. Two hours of TV was all she ever allowed Kylie and that was only on rare occasions.

"Relax, we just got back from the park. When I heard you snoring, I figured we could sneak out and let you get some rest." He shot her a teasing smirk before running off into the dining room.

"I don't snore," Ava shot after him, but she wondered if this medicine wasn't affecting her in some way. Twice, she had woken herself up with some noise from her throat before sleep overtook her again.

"How is the neck today?" Gen asked. She grabbed a few bowls from Ava's cupboard and some forks before continuing into the dining room.

"Better than yesterday, but not as good as I'd hoped. Oh, I need to tell Chris I can't come in Monday after all. The doctor said no more adjustments until the infection is gone."

"Don't worry, I'll tell Chris, but did they tell you where this infection came from?" Gen set the bowls down and doled out the forks.

Ava shrugged and scooted back a chair. "She said a sinus infection, but I didn't even know I had one."

"Well, you did have that really nasty cold thing last week that you swore was allergies. It could have been a sinus infection with as much as you blew your nose." Gen dished up Kylie's plate and put the appropriate container in front of each of the adults before taking her own seat.

"I suppose that's possible." Ava had forgotten all about the allergy troubles from the week before, but now that she thought back on them – they were worse than they ever had been. Generally, she only needed her Flonase in the morning to feel better, but that week she'd had to take her Flonase in the morning and afternoon as well as a Zyrtec in the morning. Could that have been a sinus infection instead of just allergies?

"Can we pray for Mommy to feel better?" Kylie asked.

"Of course baby, why don't you pray?" Ava smiled at her daughter before closing her eyes.

"Lord, thank you for sending Aunt Gen with the food and thank you for the nice day today so Daddy and I could have fun at the park. Please heal Mommy so she can have fun with us again too. Amen."

The adults all echoed the Amen, but the mood around the table had shifted. What if the medicine didn't work? What if Ava had to deal with this neck pain and fatigue forever? Though she knew she was blessed, at that moment all the blessings she had taken for granted flashed in her vision - the days she had woken pain free and not thanked God, the times she had been frustrated that Kylie wanted her attention when she wanted to do something else. Had this happened to make Ava take a long look at her life?

She knew the answer before she asked the question. And with that answer came the one she had been waiting on all day – the words she should share tomorrow. Ava had no idea who needed them, but they were so clear in her head that she knew they must be from God. So, neither pain nor stiffness nor exhaustion mattered. She would be on the stage tomorrow and she would share His message.

CHAPTER 7

"*H*ow are you feeling?" John asked as she stepped on the stage the next morning. He was readying the mics which was supposed to be her job as leader, but she knew that he was doing it out of kindness for her and she thanked him with a smile.

"Not completely better, but good enough to be here. Thank you for asking and thank you for helping set up."

"My pleasure. I know how pain can affect your life."

As he moved the stands to the front, his situation hit her. She'd known he had chronic pain problems, but until this week, she'd really had no idea how that must feel. Now she did, and she would never forget it.

He would be on her mind every morning in prayer and she would remember to ask how she could help him in the future.

"You feeling up to leading this?" Joyce asked as she took her place behind the piano.

"I am, and I have something I need to share. Can I talk before one of the songs?"

"Sure." Joyce pulled out the order of worship and they scanned it together. "Probably best here before Reckless Love or just after."

"I'll do it after since John is starting Reckless Love." Ava didn't really care where it went in the message. She just knew it had to be there.

The rest of the musicians and singers found their places on stage and the team ran through the songs. Then the pastor joined them on stage and they prayed for the message and for healing of Ava's neck. She hadn't taken her muscle relaxers because they made her drowsy and she could feel the heaviness in her neck creeping in already, but Ava knew she would make it through the next three hours.

As the rest of the team wandered off to use the bathroom or grab a coffee, Ava grabbed her Bible. She wanted to read something about God always being there, but she hadn't been in the Word enough lately to know which passage she wanted. After a quick Google search, she found a few verses she thought would do and when she opened her Bible to Philippians 4, she knew she had hit gold. The words not only resonated with her, but they felt right.

She closed her eyes and sent a silent prayer heavenward. "Thank you, Lord for opening my eyes this week. Thank you for making me focus on you more. Please give me the words to speak this morning that you want me to say. Shine through me today and use me as you need to."

At five minutes to nine the band began playing. Ava grabbed her Bible and opened it up to the right page. When the clock at the back showed ten seconds left, she stepped up to the mic. "Good morning church. I'm so glad you could be with us today. I'm Ava Miller, and I'll be your worship leader. Before we sing, I'd like to share some scripture with you, so if you're able, will you stand and join me in the reading of God's word? I'm reading from The Message Bible because I really like how they put it in easy to read terms, and I'm reading Philippians 4:4-10."

She took a deep breath before reading aloud the verses. "'Celebrate God all day, every day. I mean, revel in Him! Make it as clear as you can to all you meet that you're on their side, working with them and not against them. Help them see that the Master is about to arrive. He could show up any minute!

"'Don't fret or worry. Instead of worrying, pray. Let petitions and praises shape your worries into prayers, letting God know your concerns. Before you know it, a sense of God's wholeness, everything coming together for good, will come and settle you down. It's wonderful what happens when Christ displaces worry at the center of your life.

"'Summing it all up, friends, I'd say you'll do best by filling your minds and meditating on things true, noble, reputable, authentic, compelling, gracious — the best, not the worst; the beautiful, not the ugly; things to praise, not things to curse. Put into practice what you learned from me, what you heard and saw and realized. Do that, and God, who makes everything work together, will work you into his most excellent harmonies.' Amen?"

"Amen," the crowd responded and Ava led them in prayer before the singing began. Just like at practice on Thursday, Ava felt tingling in her head as she sang the praises to God. Maybe it was all in her head, but she felt like she was receiving healing as she sang on the platform, and before she knew it, they were ending Reckless Love.

Ava closed her eyes as she envisioned the words

she would say. The music softened behind her. "Before we sing this next song, I need to share something that God laid on my heart last night. See, I wasn't sure I was going to be here this morning. Earlier this week, I woke up with a soreness in my neck and by that afternoon, I couldn't move it. I thought it was just a pinched nerve, so I went to a chiropractor who thankfully sent me for x-rays before he adjusted me. Then I had another adjustment the next day and another on Friday and when I got home on Friday, the results from the x-ray were in my email inbox, and they were abnormal. So, I went to Urgent Car and after a CT scan, they found I didn't have a pinched nerve but an infection in my neck." She pointed to the spot on her neck and saw the reaction from the crowd. Some of the women had covered their mouths with their hands, but all eyes appeared firmly on her.

"And God reminded me that sin is a lot like my pain. It sneaks up on us. We do one thing thinking it's not so bad and then another and then another and before we know it, we are mired down in sin. But God is also like my doctor. When I got there Friday night, she didn't say 'Why didn't you come in Wednesday when this first happened?' No, she said 'I'm so glad you came in when you did.' And God is like that too. He's not looking to condemn us but to save us, and like we just sang, he leaves the ninety-nine to go find the one. To go find you. So, if you're here today and you don't know God because you think you've done something so terrible that He could never love you – You're wrong! And if you've distanced yourself from God because you've been mired down in sin and you think you've done something so awful that He could never forgive you – You're wrong! Because God is like that doctor. He is just waiting for us to come to Him and when we do, He doesn't say we should have come sooner. He says 'I'm glad you came when you did.' Will you join us as we sing this last song?"

If Ava thought she had felt power in the church before that song, it was nothing like the power she felt as they sang the last song. The tingling in her head was almost overpowering, but for a moment, she felt no pain and no stiffness.

"God really used you today," Joyce said as the team gathered their items together at the end of the service. "That was exactly the right thing to say and the perfect analogy."

"I agree. I was almost in tears," Alanna said coming up behind her.

"Thank you. I've never been sure I hear God

speaking to me, but when that came into my head last night, I knew it had to be Him."

"Excuse me."

Ava looked up to see a man she didn't know coming up the stairs of the stage. He was an older gentleman, probably in his late sixties or seventies with thinning white hair. "Yes, sir?"

"Can you tell me what you read today?"

"Philippians 4:4-10," Ava replied.

"Thank you," he said as he scribbled something down on a paper. "Those were exactly the words I needed to hear today along with what you said at the end."

Ava blinked at him a moment, amazed. "Thank you," she managed. She'd believed God had given her the words to say, but she didn't usually have people come and tell her they were touched.

"Seems like God had a plan for you this week," Justin said as he joined her at the base of the stage.

"Yeah, I guess so. Who would have thought a disabling neck pain would have such a profound effect?"

"I stopped questioning God's motives a long time ago," Justin said with a laugh. He took her hand as they walked down the hallway to the childcare center to retrieve Kylie.

Before they reached their car in the parking lot, three more people approached Ava thanking her for her words. Ava nodded and smiled and said 'you're welcome' with each one, but she knew she had done nothing. It had all been God.

"Mommy, is your neck better today?" Kylie asked as Ava buckled her into the car.

"It is baby, and though it's not completely healed yet, I have a feeling it will be soon."

"I know it will be," Kylie said with a smile. "God told me this morning you would be better. He just needed you to see. I thought that was silly because it was your neck that hurt and not your eyes, but do you see, Mommy?"

"I do now, bug. I do now." Ava leaned in and kissed her daughter's forehead. As she shut Kylie's door, she turned her face to the sky. "Thank you, Lord, for helping me see."

The End!

AUTHOR'S NOTE

First off, let me say how glad I am that you read this book. I struggled with what this extended epilogue should be about, but then last week, I went through this medical scare that Ava did.

I woke up with a sore neck and the next morning, it was completely stiff. The pain that she feels in this book is exactly the pain I felt and the diagnosis she received was mine.

As an update, I am now back at work. The pain has lessened though my head still feels heavy, my ear still feels intense pressure, and the back of my head still tingles. I am hopeful that after the treatment of antibiotics that the pain will go away.

Regardless, as I wrote this epilogue, I had the

realizations that Ava went through. While I wouldn't wish this pain on anyone, it did remind me of the joys I take for granted, and I hope that I will not take them for granted in the future.

And if you've enjoyed reading this author's note so far (and really, how could you not?) I am offering, for today only, a page where you can sign up for my weekly newsletter for the low, low price of absolutely nothing.

Included in this weekly newsletter are many wonderful things like pictures of my adorable children, chances to win awesome prizes, new releases and sales I might be holding, great books from other authors, and anything else that strikes my fancy and that I think you would enjoy.

Even better, I solemnly swear to only send out one newsletter a week (usually on Tuesday unless life gets in the way which with three kids it usually does). I will not spam you, sell your email address to solicitors or anyone else, or any of those other terrible things.

Join me here and receive Once Upon a Star as my thank-you gift for choosing to hang out with me. It's fun and entertaining. I promise.

Prayers and blessings,

Lorana

Ava's Blessing in Disguise is the seventh book in the multi-author Blushing Bride series, but my fourth. While each book written by a different author in the series will be a stand alone, I have decided to make mine a series. If you are reading on Amazon, the numbers may look confusing, but just know that my books will twine together. You don't have to have read The Producer's Unlikely Bride for this book to make sense, but if you have, you will have a better understanding of Justin and Ava.

With that in mind, the next book in the Blushing Bride series will be The Cop's Fiery Bride. I decided to give Cassidy her own story. Don't know who Cassidy is? Be sure to check out The Cowboy's Reality Bride.

The book will open after Cassidy returns home from being on the show. Obviously she didn't find love, but what she has found is a ton of guys trying to court her and massive teasing from her fellow firefighters.

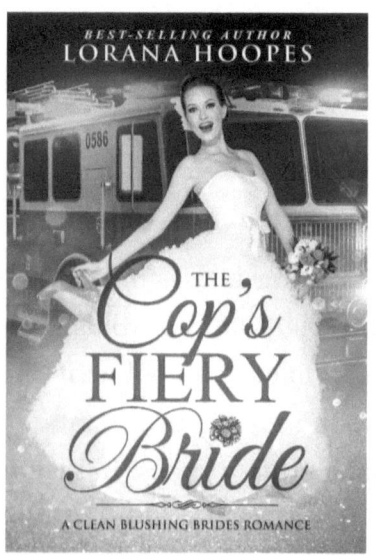

The Cop's Fiery Bride

A firefighter who just wants to get back to work.

Cassidy is glad to be back home after the reality dating show, but she did not expect so many men to be reaching out to her. Nor did she expect the teasing from her fellow firefighters. When she sees something at a fire that makes no sense, will she be able to convince anyone to take her seriously?

He's a cop who's avoided Cassidy as much as possible.

But not because he doesn't like her. Unfortunately Cassidy reminds Jordan of a painful past. However, when she sees something odd during a fire, he is forced to spend time with her to figure out what it all means

Be sure to pre-order The Cop's Fiery Bride

A FREE STORY FOR YOU

ENJOYED The Cowboy's Reality Bride? Not ready to quit reading yet? If you sign up for my newsletter, you will receive Once Upon a Star, the love story of Blake and Audrey, two of my Star Lake characters, right away as my thank you gift for choosing to hang out with me.

Once Upon a Star

A high school crush....

Blake was a nerd in high school. Never noticed. Looked over. So, it was no wonder that Audrey paid no attention to him, but now that she's back in town...

Audrey left Star Lake to pursue acting, but when she ends up pregnant and alone, she finds herself forced to return home.

Can Blake show Audrey a new side? Will she trust him enough to stay?

Read on for a taste of Once Upon a Star....

ONCE UPON A STAR PREVIEW

*A*udrey tried to peek around the nurses leaning over the silver table, obscuring the view of the thing she wanted to see most.

"Are you ready, Mom?" The head nurse, a kind, older woman with just a touch of gray in her dark hair, turned to Audrey, a tiny blue package in her arms.

Mom. The word had never applied to her, and she wasn't sure it fit. Was she ready? Probably not. Would she ever be completely ready? Probably not. But that didn't change reality. She tucked a strand of blond hair behind her ear and nodded.

"Here's your son." The nurse held the swaddled bundle out to her. Audrey opened her hands, unsure of what the nurse wanted her to do. The nurse's face softened and her warm brown eyes sparkled. With one hand, she adjusted Audrey's arms to place the tiny bundle in them. "Hold him like this." She demonstrated the proper technique. "You always want to support his head."

Audrey nodded, trying to keep her arms from shaking. She was afraid to breathe, afraid to move, but mostly afraid she'd drop the infant, so she kept her eyes glued to him. Would he shatter like a piece of glass? The image sent a shiver down her spine. She didn't want to find out.

The nurse's eyes twinkled as she watched Audrey adjust and readjust her holding position. "There is a bassinet here." She pointed at a clear plastic tub that looked like a large shoe box on top of a wheeled table. It didn't look comfortable to Audrey, and she wondered how a baby slept in it. "If you want to take him walking, you need to put him in the bassinet, okay?"

"Do I hold him the rest of the time?" As much as she was enjoying the baby in her arms, what happened when she needed to sleep or use the bathroom?

The woman chuckled. "You hold him as much as you want and put him down when you need a break. We'll come in every few hours to check on you, and we'll show you how to change his diaper and dress him. You'll be a pro before you know it. Don't worry." She patted Audrey's arm like her grandmother used to when she asked a silly question, and then the nurse walked out of the room, still smiling and shaking her head.

Audrey's eyes dropped to the sleeping baby. His shock of dark hair reminded her of his father, the olive-skinned Italian who had charmed her with his fast tongue. She hoped it was the only trait Cayden would get from him. The world didn't need another heartbreaker. "I have no idea what we'll do, Cayden, but we'll figure something out."

BLAKE TURNED the glass on the countertop and glanced up at Max who leaned against the back counter, arms folded across his chest as if he were waiting for the answer to a question. The green of his plaid shirt matched the faded ball cap turned backwards on his head. "Sorry, did you say something? I'm distracted; it's just getting close to Christmas, and I miss Connie." A vision of the day she left popped into his head.

Blake opened the door, expecting to see Connie on the other side in her Sunday best. The church service started in half an hour. Though Connie stood there, his smile faded as he took in her jeans and t-shirt. There was no requirement of the patrons to dress up, but Connie always wore a dress or skirt. "What's going on?" Blake asked.

Connie bit her lip and her eyes fell to the ground. "I wanted to say goodbye."

"Goodbye?"

"I can't stay any longer, Blake." Her eyes lifted to meet his, and he saw the shimmer of liquid in them. "I hoped I could make a life here, but I'm a city girl. I miss the lights and night life. I miss the excitement."

"But, we were discussing marriage last week." Blake struggled to make her words compute in his brain.

"I know," she nodded, "and that's what got me thinking. The thought of living the rest of my life here is depressing, so though I love you, I have to say goodbye." She leaned in and pecked his cheek before flashing a sad smile and walking back to her car.

With a heavy heart, Blake watched her drive away before shutting the door and leaning against it. His brain tried to make sense of her departure.

"I GET IT," Max said, leaning forward and dispersing Blake's memory. "It's not the same, but you're welcome to spend Christmas with Layla and me.

Blake offered a half smile. "I'll consider it, but it's your first Christmas together. You've been in love with that woman since I've known you and I don't want to be a third wheel. Besides, I'll probably hit the Christmas Eve service at church and spend the day with my mom. She's been lonely without my father around."

Max shrugged and turned back to the kitchen to finish serving the lunch crowd.

Blake took a bite of his hamburger, but while he knew it was delicious—Max was known for his burgers—it held no taste in his current mood. He fished a few dollars out of his wallet, laid the money on the counter, picked up his coat, and walked out the door.

The McAllister development where he worked sat a mile up the road, but as he still had fifteen minutes remaining on his lunch break, he decided to walk through downtown. His own house resided on the quiet outskirts of town, so other than hanging out with Max at The Diner, he didn't spend much time in the downtown area.

Blake pulled his coat tighter as the winter air bit through the heavy wool. Star Lake generally received one or two good snowfalls every winter, and though Christmas was still a few weeks away, the chill in the air made him believe the first snow was coming.

He didn't mind the snow, but he enjoyed it more when he had someone to share the experience with. Curling in front of the fireplace alone held little appeal.

AUDREY SHOVED the last item in her suitcase and pushed down on the bulging bag as she tugged on the zipper.

"Where are you going to go?" Desiree asked, leaning against the doorframe.

Desiree was Audrey's roommate, and the two were about as different as night and day. Where Audrey was pale and blond, Desiree had darker skin and long dark hair.

"The only place I can," Audrey said with a sigh. "Home."

The thought held little appeal. Her wealthy parents had given her access to her trust fund at eighteen, and Audrey had opted to move to LA to try her hand at acting. At first, it had been fun. She'd found a few jobs and been in a few commercials, but then the jobs had become fewer and farther between, and after she ended up pregnant, they had dried up completely. Now all the money she had saved was almost gone.

Desiree's nose scrunched in disgust. "You'd go back to that tiny town, why?"

"I haven't had a job in months Dez, my savings have run out, and I can't go to work without someone to watch Cayden. If I go home, I can get help from my parents until I get back on my feet."

At least she hoped they would help. They hadn't been too happy when she decided not to go to college, but she didn't think they would turn their grandson away, even if they didn't want to help her.

Desiree shrugged and flicked her hair behind her bony shoulder. "Nothing in the world would make me return to my crappy hometown."

Audrey knew Desiree's home life had been rough, but while she hadn't wanted to grow up under her mother's thumb, it hadn't been a bad childhood. "I don't know if I'll ever be back, but I wish you luck."

After a quick hug, Audrey picked up Cayden's car seat, slung her bag over her shoulder, and left the apartment she had called home for the last few years.

Click here to sign up for my newsletter and continue reading Once Upon a Star.

THE STORY DOESN'T END!

You've met a few people and fallen in love....

I bet you're wondering how you can meet everyone else.

Star Lake Series:
When Love Returns
Once Upon a Star
Love Conquers All
Heartbeats Series:
Where It All Began
The Power of Prayer
When Hearts Collide
A Past Forgiven
Sweet Billionaires Series:

The Billionaire's Secret

Brush with a Billionaire

The Billionaire's Christmas Miracle

The Billionaire's Cowboy Groom

The Lawkeepers series:

Lawfully Matched

Lawfully Justified

The Scarlet Wedding

Lawfully Redeemed

Lawfully Pursued

Still Small Voice series:

The Still Small Voice

A Spark in the Darkness (coming soon)

Stand Alones:

Love Renewed

Blushing Brides Series:

The Cowboy's Reality Bride

The Reality Bride's Baby

The Producer's Unlikely Bride

Her children's early reader chapter book series:

The Wishing Stone #1: Dangerous Dinosaur

The Wishing Stone #2: Dragon Dilemma

The Wishing Stone #3: Mesmerizing Mermaids

The Wishing Stone #4: Pyramid Puzzles

The Wishing Stone Inspirations #1: Mary's Miracle

To see a list of all her books

authorloranahoopes.com
loranahoopes@gmail.com

WOULD YOU LEAVE A REVIEW?

As an author, I highly appreciate the feedback I get from my readers. It helps others make an informed decision before buying my book.

If you've enjoyed this story, please be sure to leave a review at your retailer.

Do you like free books? I'm offering a free sample of my next book Free Sample!

ABOUT THE AUTHOR

Lorana Hoopes is an inspirational author originally from Texas but now living in the PNW with her husband and three children. When not writing, she can be seen kickboxing at the gym, singing, or acting on stage. One day, she hopes to retire from teaching and write full time.

www.ingramcontent.com/pod-product-compliance
Lightning Source LLC
Chambersburg PA
CBHW020636130626
46552CB00003B/1259